# Say You'll Remember Me

**Say You'll Remember Me, Volume 1**

DeJane Penick

Published by DeJane Penick, 2022.

SAY YOU'LL REMEMBER ME

**First edition. August 11, 2022.**

Copyright © 2022 DeJane Penick.

ISBN: 979-8215627044

Written by DeJane Penick.

# Table of Contents

I dedicate this book to my family, my friends, and most importantly, my lovely characters.

# Say You'll Remember Me

# Prologue

There are many theories about the afterlife. Some believe that there is a Heaven and Hell, that if you're good then you'll be rewarded but if you're bad, then you'll be tortured for all eternity. Other people believe that there is no afterlife and we'll just be in the ground decaying away, not feeling anything ever again. My parents believed in both of these theories. But I believe that our souls walk around the earth as ghosts until we figure out our unfinished business and move on. I know because I can see them. I've been able to see ghosts since I was five years old but I've never actually talked to or felt one. My parents thought I was insane when I told them. We weren't close anyway. But I never thought that I would help one, let alone fall in love with one.

# Chapter One

My name is Michael Wilson and according to my whole family, I'm a psychopath. Since I was little, I've been able to see ghosts. Every time I saw one, I would always run to my parents crying but they never believed me. My mom would always fight with my dad about sending me to an asylum or mental institution. My dad finally had enough and left us. He left me with her. He's probably with his new family in a beautiful house with a white picket fence like normal people. But after he left, there was no one to protect me from her anymore so she finally got her wish. I stayed in a mental hospital for six months and was never the same again. After I turned 18, I moved out of there as fast as possible into my own apartment.

After that, I didn't see any ghosts so maybe it was in my head. Anyway, I went into my apartment with my groceries and put them on the table. Today is my girlfriend, Chloe and I's six-month anniversary. I met her at my job two years ago and unlike the other people there, she was nice to me. She has dark brown eyes and bright blonde hair. She's on the short side but then again I'm almost six feet tall so everyone's shorter than me.

I checked my messages and there were five new messages from my Mom. I blocked her five times already. I don't want to talk to her again. Then, I saw a new message from Chloe.

*Hey, I'm not going to make it to dinner tonight*

> *Ok, we can always celebrate our anniversary tmmr*

*Actually, can we talk at my place?*

> *Sure*
>
> **Read at 10:04 am*

I wonder what she wants to talk about.

I got out of the car after I got to her house. I knocked on the door and waited. I checked my phone on what the weather was going to be like for this week and it was supposed to rain the whole time. I mentally sighed. Seattle.

Chloe finally opened the door but it was clear that she had been crying.

"Hey, what's wro-?"

She cut me off by hugging me and started crying. I immediately hugged her back.

"What happened," I asked softly.

She pulled away and looked up at me.

"My ex-boyfriend, Paris, his sister just called me and told me that he's dead."

# Chapter Two

After Chloe had calmed down, we went inside and sat on the couch. I gave her some tissues and she silently thanked me.

"She said that he overdosed while he was in South Korea."

"South Korea?"

"He's a-. **Was** a photographer and his last job was in Korea."

"Oh, were you guys still close before he left?"

"Yeah, we broke up months before he left but we still texted and stuff like that. But then three days ago he stopped, probably partying. He was an addict to alcohol and drugs before we met. It took him six months to stop. I should've known that leaving him alone would-."

"Hey, it's not your fault. When's the funeral?"

"Either Thursday or Friday. They have to fly his body back out here and then his mom has to get everything situated. I'm sorry we can't celebrate our anniversary."

"Don't even worry about it. We can celebrate next week or the week after that. Whenever you're ready."

She smiled at me and pinched my cheeks.

"You're so sweet. Thank you for understanding."

Her phone started ringing.

"That's Phoenix, his sister. I gotta take this."

"I'll be here."

She left while talking to Phoenix. It sucks that we have to postpone our anniversary but her and this Paris guy were close so it's probably super hard on her. I looked around her house but then my eyes caught something out the window. It was a Korean girl that looked about my age. But something else caught my eye. It looked like her throat had been slit. She just continued to stare at me making my breathing pick up. I thought it was finally over.

"Michael?"

I turned to look at Chloe.

"You okay?"

I looked back at the window and the girl was gone. Maybe I am crazy.

# Chapter Three

Friday came faster than I wanted it to. I went to that Paris kid's funeral for Chloe. I drew a shaky breath after it was over. I hate funerals. Obviously, there are a bunch of ghosts because some families put out food for their dead loved ones. Speaking of that food, I saw a girl steal some and a little ghost boy glared at her.

"The ghosts don't like that."

"Ghosts don't exist and I'm pretty sure my brother won't mind me stealing some food."

"Oh, you're Phoenix?"

"Yeah and I'm guessing you're Michael, Chloe's boyfriend who is only here to make her happy."

"Well yeah, I'm her-."

"Boyfriend, I know," she said, annoyed.

She seems like she doesn't like me. I decided to leave her alone and go up to the body. This was my first time seeing Paris and honestly, he was kinda cute. He had wavy brunette hair that went to the side and a small thin nose. He was paler than a vampire, well he's dead so obviously, he's pale. Then, I saw there was a thin hole in his hand. Did he stab himself?

"He's beautiful isn't he?"

I turned around and saw a middle-aged woman with bags under her eyes.

"Um, yeah. I'm Michael, Chloe's boyfriend," I said, holding out my hand.

"Sydney, I'm Paris's mother," she said, shaking my hand.

"Oh, I'm sorry about-."

"It's fine. I'm happy you're here, you seem like a nice guy."

Chloe went up to me and held my hand.

"Ms. Walker, they're about to do the burial."

"Okay, thanks, sweetie."

She walked away. But then I saw a bunch of ghosts hanging around glaring at me making me hyperventilate.

"You okay baby?"

"Yeah, I just need some air."

I quickly left and went outside to a bench. I took a deep breath and let it out. I laid my head back and closed my eyes. After a few moments, I felt someone sit next to me. Probably Chloe. I opened my eyes and looked to my side to see a guy my age with piercing blue eyes and pale skin. He looks familiar.

"Um hello?"

"Hey, I'm Paris."

# Chapter Four

My name is Paris and I'm dead. One minute I was in South Korea and then I was back in Seattle. I looked down at my body. At least they put me in a cute tuxedo. I walked out and saw a tall guy sitting alone on a bench. I sat next to him and he was cute up close. He had straight blonde hair that almost covered his eyes and he had freckles on his nose. He opened his eyes and looked at me confused. Thank God there's another ghost here.

"Um, hello?"

"Hey, I'm Paris."

He still looked confused but all of a sudden his eyes widened and he groaned.

"Okay, that was rude. I thought people were nicer in the afterlife."

I looked over at them loading my coffin into the hearse. I quickly looked away not wanting to see myself on the way to being buried.

"Hey, you wanna walk around?"

"Sure, you seem more annoying than scary."

"Ouch."

We stood up and walked around the park.

"You never told me your name, stranger."

He sighed.

"Michael."

"Mind if I call you Mikey?"

"Very."

"You know, I would never do this if I was alive. If someone walked up to me and started talking to me I would most likely flip them off and walk away. But now I've decided to be nicer."

"Good for you."

"I'm starting to regret that decision," I said through my teeth.

"Sorry, I shouldn't take my anger out on you."

"No shit," I mumbled.

He rolled his eyes and we crossed the street. Then I saw a car coming.

'LOOK OUT!"

I pushed him out of the way and I waited for the impact. I opened my eyes as the car went right through me. Oh right. The car stopped and a lady got out. She ran to Michael who was still on the ground. Can she see him?

# Chapter Five

After he reassured the woman that he was okay, she got back in her car and drove away. He turned around and screeched when he saw me.

"So you're alive?"

"Very."

"Then, how can you see me?"

"I've just been able to see ghosts when I was young. I don't know how and I don't wanna know why," he said walking away.

"If you're alive then why were you at my funeral, also was it good? Did they get Ariana Grande to sing," I asked following him.

"I was there for Chloe, it was long, and no they didn't, they got your cousin to sing."

"Ugh, she always sounds like a dying cat when she sings. Wait, why would you be there for Chloe?"

"Because she's my girlfriend."

"Ouch and gross. How did I die?"

"Wow, you really love asking questions."

"I just want to know what cut my life short."

He stopped in his tracks making me stop.

"You don't remember?"

"Am I supposed to?"

He was about to say something when his phone rang. He checked it and sighed.

"It's Chloe, I gotta go."

"Wait, how did I die?!"

"You overdosed in South Korea, bye!"

He walked away leaving me alone. Did I overdose? Why can't I remember and why would I overdose? I was sober when I left but I can't remember my last day. I ran my fingers through my hair and turned toward a car window and realized that I couldn't even see my reflection. Great, I can't even see how good I look! I turned around and bumped into someone.

"Sor-."

I stopped talking and screamed when I saw a Korean girl with her neck slit staring at me. I cleared my throat.

"I mean hello totally normal girl, do I know you?"

She grabbed my hand and closed her eyes.

"Okay?"

Suddenly, there was a flash of light making me close my eyes. When I opened them we were somewhere else.

"Where are we and how did we get here? Are you magic?"

She looked at me annoyed.

"???."

"Korea," I asked since she was speaking Korean.

My eyes widened.

"Wait, are we in good Korea or bad Korea?"

She glared at me.

"Sorry."

"???? ????? ? ????."

Okay, I definitely didn't understand that.

"We can teleport as ghosts," she said in English.

"Oh. You can speak English?"

"I was a model."

"So you had to learn English. Okay, why are we here?"

She pointed at an apartment building. Then, I remembered that I used to live there.

"This is my apartment building, I died here didn't I?"

She nodded.

"There's no way I overdosed, I wouldn't do that and why can't I remember my death? Can you remember yours?"

"All I remember is someone coming up from behind and…"

She mimics cutting her throat. I nodded and looked back at the building. I went through the door and went to my apartment. I looked beside me and the girl was still there.

"Are you Casper the ghost or something? Why are you following me?"

"Haha, my soul is connected to yours for some reason."

"Maybe we're soulmates," I said, putting my arm around her shoulders.

She scoffed and pushed it off.

"Worth a shot. You still haven't told me your name."

"Kim Mi-Cha."

"I'm gonna call you Mimi."

"Please don't."

"That's how I remember names."

We went through the door and my apartment was surprisingly clean.

"Well, there's definitely something wrong because I never clean my apartment. I didn't even make my bed at home."

"If they said you overdosed then you most likely died in…"

"My room or the bathroom."

We went to my room and it was also clean.

"Okay, no one's room is this clean," Mi-Cha said.

"I know, it's like-."

Suddenly, I tripped over something and fell on the bed. Mi-Cha giggled.

"It's not funny, I almost died a second time!"

"You fell on your bed."

"But what if I didn't?"

"Oh no you almost fell two feet," she said sarcastically.

Then, I looked at the floor. I tripped over the carpet but there was a red stain on the edge of it. The whole apartment floor is made out of wood except for the carpet surrounding the bed.

"Is that blood?"

"They did say you stabbed your hand."

"But that doesn't make any sense. How can I be high enough to stab my hand and then overdose, unless...someone else stabbed it."

"Paris."

She pointed to the rest of the carpet. The edge was also red but fading like someone tried to wash it off. The trail led to the bathroom. We went inside and the bathroom was spotless but then my head started to hurt.

*I tried to get out of the person's grip as they dragged me by my hair to the tub full of water. Then, they shoved my head in. I struggled to get them off my head. They repeatedly dunked my head in until I could barely breathe anymore and dark spots clouded my vision. Then, everything was black.*

# Chapter Six

"Well it was a beautiful funeral," Chloe said.

A long, boring funeral.

"Where'd you go after?"

"I just went for a little walk. Sorry for not telling you."

"It's okay. Do you want something to drink?"

"Yeah."

"Cool, the water's in the fridge," she said, sitting down and getting on her phone.

I rolled my eyes and went to her kitchen. I opened the fridge and grabbed a water bottle. I opened it and started drinking when I saw Paris pressed up against the glass staring at me. I spit out my water and started coughing.

"Babe are you okay?"

"Fine, I just need air, again."

I hurried outside and went up to Paris and the girl from before.

"Why are you here and who is she?"

"This is Mi-Cha, my soulmate."

"We are not."

"And I'm here because we need your help."

"Help with what?"

"I didn't overdose in Korea, I was murdered."

"How do you know?"

"Well someone pushing my head underwater purposely was a big part of it, Mikey," Paris said annoyed.

I can see what he meant by trying to be nicer.

"What does this have to do with me?"

"You're a living, breathing human who can see ghosts. Meaning that you can help us solve our murder."

"Yeah, no."

I started walking back to the house when he grabbed my arm.

"You have to help us, you're the only one who can see us, and even when we find out who murdered us how are we gonna get them arrested and for suspects, how are we gonna talk to them and find out where they were and detective stuff like that?"

"This isn't Scooby-Doo. I hate ghosts and I always will. Now leave me alone."

He glared at me.

"Alright, you leave me no choice. I will haunt you until you say yes."

"Oh please. If you're gonna start flickering the lights, or writing on the mirror, or any other paranormal activity stuff then it's not gonna work because I've been dealing with that since I was five. So goodbye Casper and Stretch."

"Hey, I already said that joke!"

"Well I said it better," I said walking away.

I went back inside with them following me and sat next to Chloe.

"Do you want to watch something on Netflix?"

"Sure. What do you wanna watch?"

"We could watch Love Alarm?"

"No Kdramas please."

"Why? You'll need to learn Korean when you go to Korea," Paris said.

I hissed at him.

"How about Dead To Me?"

"You'll be dead to us if you don't do this," Paris said, getting closer.

I shivered.

"Nothing about dead people or the word dead in the title either."

"There goes half my list. We can watch Ariana Grande's documentary."

"Say yes, SAY YES," Paris yelled.

"Not really a fan of Ariana," I said, getting annoyed.

"Well Paris was and we can watch it in his memory."

"Yeah, because I'll always be in her memory and I'll always be in yours," he whispered in my ear.

"FINE! I'LL DO IT!"

Chloe looked at me confused and scared.

"I mean, I'll watch the documentary."

"Yay," she said smiling.

I weakly smiled back and glared at Paris who was smirking. How hard can it be to solve two murders?

# Chapter Seven

"How am I supposed to pay for stuff if they don't take American money," I asked Paris and Mi-Cha.

"Just go to a Global ATM and it'll give you Korean money, it has to be global, or else it won't work."

"One week. If we don't figure it out by then, then I quit."

"Deal."

I put my credit card in and transferred 500 dollars into Korean money. I took it and went to a hotel.

"Mi-Cha, what hotel will let me stay for a week for 1,122 won?"

"Why are you speaking to her like she's Siri," Paris asked.

"Nowhere because you're only holding a dollar."

"Great, glad I spent 500 dollars on a dollar," I said sarcastically.

We walked down the sidewalk.

"Alright, we should probably retrace your footsteps."

"I don't remember."

"What do you remember?"

"Someone dragged me to my bathtub and drowned me."

"Maybe someone broke in. Did you have any enemies?"

"Well..."

"That means he has a long list," Mi-Cha said.

"Okay, who do you think would kill you knowing you were staying here?"

"My ex-fling, Dong-Hyun."

I raised my eyebrow.

"Don't be homophobic," he said annoyed.

"I'm not, I'm cool with that but why him?"

"We were an on and off thing while I was here. But Chloe wouldn't leave us alone and of course, that made him mad."

"Wait, what do you mean Chloe wouldn't leave you alone?"

"We broke up last week but she always called and texted me to get back together."

She tried to get back together with him while she was with me.

"Chloe told me, you guys broke up months ago."

"No, I broke up with her because she was a psycho."

That made all of us stop. Paris turned to me.

"No," I said firmly.

"She also knew I was here."

"Anyone can be a suspect," Mi-Cha said.

"Chloe wouldn't do that."

"Well, I guess we'll find out."

He disappeared.

"Wait, where's he-?"

Mi-Cha grabbed my hand and there was a flash of light. I fell to the ground and looked around. We were suddenly in front of an apartment building with Paris waiting for us. I stood up stumbling.

"Please don't ever do that again. Where are we?"

"This is my apartment building."

I looked around and saw something metal on the ground. It looks like a car part.

"Okay so-."

Mi-Cha gasped and disappeared.

"Where'd she go?"

"I don't know."

I looked around to see what could've scared her off when I saw a girl my age walking toward us on her phone.

"Do you know her?"

Paris looked at her.

"No. Do you think she's Mi-Cha's sister?"

"I don't..."

I stopped talking when she walked past us. She looked up and smiled at me. Then, she frowned when she looked Paris's way. Just like that, she walked away.

"What the-," Paris said breathed out.

"Could she see you?"

"I don't know. Let's just go inside."

Paris went inside and I was about to follow him but I turned around to see the girl staring at us. Who is she?

# Chapter Eight

I picked the lock at the door and opened it so Michael could come in.

"Ta-da!"

"Wow, I'm so impressed," Michael said sarcastically.

I rolled my eyes as he came in.

"Is Mi-Cha in here?"

"No, why? Do you have a crush on her," I asked teasingly.

"I have a girlfriend."

"Still. Anyway, look around my sweet home."

He nodded and looked at the door.

"The door looks brand new like someone replaced it. They must've broken in, killed you, and then replaced the door."

"Okay, Sherlock, why would a robber go through all that trouble?"

"I don't know. Maybe it wasn't a robber."

He went up to me and gently grabbed my chin. I blushed.

"W-What are you doing," I stuttered out.

"Looking for any bruises. If you guys kept your injuries then they'll be something that'll show that they beat you up."

I avoided looking into his eyes as he looked me over. He removed his hand from my chin and went to my hair.

"There's a gash here. They must've hit something against you, knocking you out, and then drowned you."

"What about my hand then?"

"Hm, maybe you did stab yourself."

I punched him in the arm.

"It's a theory!"

I went back to my room with him following me.

"Did you have your phone on you?"

"I don't think so, plus if phones work in horror movies then every movie would be two minutes long."

"Maybe you left it at your workplace."

"Yeah, it could've been daytime when I died."

I grabbed his hand.

"Oh God."

"You'll get used to it."

I transported us to my workplace.

"Do you think it could've been your boss?"

"No, he treated me like a son, besides he said that he and Jin-Ae were going on a date that day."

"Who's Jin-Ae?"

I looked at him annoyed.

"His dog who else would be going on a date with him," I said sarcastically.

"Well sorry. What does she do?"

"She owns the cafe that I usually go to..."

We looked at each other.

"The cafe," we said in unison.

I was about to grab his hand when he pulled away.

"Can't we just walk?"

"Ugh fine."

We left and started walking when we saw my boss, Hyun's car. The front bumper was about to come off.

"What happened to his car?"

"I don't know."

We continued walking until we were at the cafe after thirty minutes.

"Wait, the cafe is five minutes away from your apartment?!"

"Yeah, that's why I come here every day."

"Well, why didn't you just poof us to the apartment building?!"

"You said not to!"

He sighed.

"Whatever, let's just-."

He stopped himself and went into an alleyway. I was curious as to why he was going that way and followed him. He knelt down and picked up something. He turned around and showed me a cracked phone with dry blood on it. Then, a realization hit me when he turned it on revealing the background of me and Phoenix.

"I think this is yours."

# Chapter Nine

"Here's some coffee dear."

"Thanks, Jin-Ae."

"Can I have some coffee," Paris asked annoyed.

I waited until she walked away to glare at him.

"You're a ghost, you can't drink coffee. Is your phone charged yet?"

"It's at 15%."

"Close enough."

"So someone didn't break in or follow me home. I was chased."

Mi-Cha appeared in the chair next to us, making us yell. Jin-Ae looked at me confused.

"Coffee burned my tongue," I said, sending her an awkward smile.

I got out my phone and put in my earbuds so it looked like I was on the phone.

"Where were you?"

"I went to my house."

"What did you find?"

"Nothing but an empty house as usual. Did you guys find anything?"

"We found Paris's phone in an alleyway."

"And the last person that called me was Chloe."

"What about the last person who texted you?"

"Um, my sister."

He showed us the texts

*When r u coming home?*

*I can't stand mom's new boyfriend*

   *Don't worry I'm about to get on my plane.*

*I miss u and ur stupid face*

*Aight, luv u jerk*

*Luv u too psycho*

*Hey, my flight got canceled so I'm going to be here for another two days*

*Srry, luv u :-(*

**Read at 7:06 am**

"You were about to go home but your flight got canceled."

"Maybe my death was set up. Mi-Cha, where's your phone?"

"I don't know, it wasn't at my house or my workplace."

"Maybe the person who murdered you stole it."

I thought of something.

"Or maybe it's still where your body was found. What's the address?"

She told me the address and I put it into Google Maps.

"Alright I have the address, let's go," I said standing up.

"Honey, are you okay?"

"Yeah, why?"

"Because you were saying "Let's go" to nobody."

"Oh um, I'm playing a game with my friend online."

"Oh okay. Well come back, we're open from seven am to nine pm!"

We ran out the door and to the address. Only to find a bridge.

"That's where they found your body huh."

"Yep."

"So your phone is most likely all the way down in the ocean?"

"Yep."

"Nothing is ever easy is it."

# Chapter Ten

"Oh quit whining, I'll get it."

I went up to the water.

"Be careful," Michael said.

"Mikey, I'm dead, what's gonna happen? I become even deader?"

I dived into the water and looked around. Even though I miss breathing, I'm kinda glad I can't anymore. I swam to the very bottom and saw something shiny. Mi-Cha said her phone case has rhinestones on it and is pink. I grabbed it and was about to swim back up when something grabbed my leg. I looked down and my scream was muffled by the water. A ghost-skeleton girl was hanging onto my leg.

"...Save...me."

I tried to get it off me but she continued clinging on, digging her nails into my leg. She screamed as she started clawing at me. I dodged her attacks and punched them, knocking them off. Then, a bunch of skeleton ghosts came out and started charging toward me. I quickly swam to the surface with them following me. All of them grabbed at my legs, trying to pull me under but Michael grabbed my arm while Mi-Cha grabbed my other arm. They pulled until it finally let go and I was out of the water.

"What the hell was that?!"

"Those are the ghosts of the people who committed suicide or were murdered here and haven't moved on for three years. They can't leave the water and try to pull down any human or ghost down there with them."

"Why?"

"A life for a life."

I shivered.

"Here's your phone, let's get out of here before the Loch Ness Monster comes out."

"Wait, I have to go to the store and get some rice to put this in."

"I can just steal it."

"Paris do-."

I transported to a nearby store before he could finish. I looked around for the rice and smiled when I saw it. I grabbed it and smirked.

"Easy peasy."

I turned around to transport when I saw the girl from before staring at me.

"So you can see me."

"You're a ghost?"

"Well I'm not a vampire," I said sarcastically.

"I'm Kim Bong."

"...you're Mi-Cha's sister."

"You know her?"

"Yeah we're super close," I said sarcastically while walking away.

"Did she say who murdered her?"

I stopped in my tracks. I turned around and went back up to her.

"You know it was a murder too."

"There's no way that she committed suicide. She wouldn't do that to our parents and Sung-Ho."

"Who's Sung-Ho?"

"Her boyfriend. She said she was meeting him the night she died."

"Meeting him where?"

"The cafe."

Wait. That's where I dropped my phone which was covered in blood.

"Do you think that he killed her?"

"He was meeting her."

"I think that he did but I got in the way."

"What do you mean?"
"Because I was there too."

# Chapter Eleven

"What is taking Paris so long with the-?"

I screeched as Paris appeared with a girl.

"Where were you?"

"This is Bong, Mi-Cha's sister."

I noticed that Bong and Mi-Cha were glaring at each other. Paris stood by me.

"It's like we're in a lion's den."

"Mi-Cha, you're here."

"Why wouldn't I be," Mi-Cha asked sneeringly.

"We should leave them alone," I whispered.

"No way, this is better than Dance Moms."

"Why are you mad at me?"

"Oh, so you don't remember what you said to me last time we talked."

"Mi-Cha-."

"It's not my fault that mom and dad like me better than you."

Bong glared at her.

"Damn," Paris said.

They started arguing in Korean. It reminded me of my parents arguing. Over me. My breathing started picking up. I walked away and started running down the street. I laid back against a wall, my thoughts not leaving me. I slid down the wall covering my ears.

*"Disappointment."*

*"Useless."*

*"Psycho."*

*"I would rather die than have you as a son!"*

"Michael!"

I looked up and saw Paris with his hand on my shoulder.

"You okay?"

My breathing went back to normal as I focused on him and only him.

"Yeah, I'm okay."

"Why'd you run away?"

"I'm just in my head. Why'd you follow me?"

"I didn't want you to be alone."

We stared into each other's eyes for a while before I stood up with him following.

"Bong and Mi-Cha's argument. About their last conversation. It made me think about my mom."

"What about her?"

"When I left for Korea, we had an argument and I never got to say goodbye. While I was here, I wrote her a letter and I was going to mail it but I was scared to. So I was wondering if..."

He pulled out a letter.

"Yeah of course."

"Cool."

He grabbed my hand and transported us somewhere.

"WAIT NOW?!"

"Look, if we do find out who murdered me and Mi-Cha then...I don't know what will happen. I need to do this while I'm here."

He was looking at me with hopeful eyes. I sighed.

"Five minutes and we go back to Korea."

I knocked on the door and waited. Sydney opened the door.

"Oh, Michael you're here."

"Yeah, can I come in?"

"Not at all."

I came in with Paris right behind me. She closed the door as I went to the center of the living room.

"Did you want some tea?"

"Um, actually, I came to talk about Paris."

"What about Paris?"

I got out Paris's letter and gave it to her.

"Paris wrote this to you."

She gave me a confused look.

"I found it...somewhere."

She nodded and opened it.

*Dear Mom,*

*I hate how we last things. I just want to go back in time and reverse the things I did to make us not fight anymore and to reverse the pain I gave you after I left. I know I should've turned around when I ran out but I had too much pride. I didn't even get to apologize. The words we said in our fight are going to stay in my mind forever. I want to fix things between us but I feel helpless and trapped like there's a barrier between us. I wish I could rewrite our fight so I can replace all the angry words with "I love you." Maybe then you won't forget me. If you could only know that I'd never let you go. And the words I most regret are the ones I never meant to leave*

*Love, Paris*

By the end, Sydney and Paris were crying. I noticed that I was crying too and wiped my eyes. She looked at me with tears in her eyes.

"Thank you."

"You're welcome. I know he was only 23 when he...but he loves you and he wants you to be happy."

I heard a whoosh behind me and knew that Paris left. I said goodbye and looked around for him. I found him at a bridge. I stood next to him as we stayed silent.

"It was a beautiful letter."

"Thanks."

We stood there in silence again.

"Leaving my mom was probably one of the biggest regrets in my life, so again thank you. I mean it."

He hugged me and I hesitantly hugged back. I know we've only known each other for two or three days but, I would do anything for Paris.

# Chapter Twelve

We decided to walk around before going back to Korea.

"Being a ghost sucks," I said, breaking the silence.

"That came out of nowhere. Why?"

"When I came back as a ghost at first, I was confused and was back home."

*I walked home with my hair wet for some reason. How did I get back from Korea so fast? I went to open the door but my hand went through. What the hell? I tried again and I opened it this time. Am I still tired from the flight? I'm probably hallucinating. I went inside and saw my mom cooking.*

*"Hey, I'm back."*

*She ignored me.*

*"I'm sorry for arguing with you, I didn't mean it," I said sitting on the stool.*

*Then, the phone rang. She answered it.*

*"Hello?"*

*I tapped my fingers on the table. I looked up and saw her covering her mouth. She started sobbing.*

*"Mom, what's wrong," I asked, panicking.*

*Phoenix came in.*

*"Mom, what happened?"*

*"Your brother...he's dead."*

*My heart dropped.*

*"No, I'm not, I'm right here!"*

*Phoenix started crying and I went to her.*

*"Phoenix, I'm right here."*

*I turned towards mom and she was heading towards Phoenix.*

*"Mom I'm right her-!"*

*She went through me and I went speechless.*

*"M-Mom?"*

*I tried to touch her but my hand went through. I backed up into the counter hyperventilating.*

*"Come on, we have to call your aunt."*

*"No, you don't! Mom, I'm right here! MOM!"*

*She couldn't hear me and I collapsed to the floor sobbing.*

*"I'm right here," I choked out.*

"I hated that day."

"I'm sorry you went through that Paris."

"I'm just glad that you gave her my letter."

"She seems like a nice lady."

"She is. What's your mom like?"

He stopped in his tracks.

"She's not dead, is she? If she is, I'm sorry I brought it up."

"She's not. She's just...nothing like your mom."

"What do you mean?"

*I WENT INSIDE AND TOOK off my shoes.*

*"I'm home!"*

*There was no answer. I sighed and took my bookbag off. I went to my room while passing my parent's room when I noticed my mom staring at the wall while smoking. I went inside confused.*

*"Are you okay, mom?"*

*"Your father left."*

*"For work?"*

*"No."*

*I gave her a confused look.*

*"Mom, where is he?"*

*"He left us."*

*"What-?"*

*"He left because of you!"*

*She came towards me, making me back away.*

*"All because of your stupid little ghost stories! You should be gone, not him! And now he's living with that slut while I'm stuck here with you!"*

*"Mom, I'm sorry," I said, tearing up.*

*"Sorry? You're always just sorry, aren't you? Well, you're gonna be sorry once I'm through with you."*

*She grabbed my arm and burned her cigarette into it making me scream in agony.*

"Michael?"

I looked at him and didn't realize we stopped.

"Nothing, let's just go back to Korea."

"Okay. Are you-?"

"I'm fine, let's just go."

He looked unsure but nodded and grabbed my hand. Just forget those memories.

# Chapter Thirteen

I transported us back to Korea and we walked back to the park. It was night time so barely anyone was out.

"Did you wanna talk about what happened earlier? With your panic attack?"

He sighed.

"You know how I can see ghosts right?"

"Obviously or else we wouldn't be talking right now."

"Well, when I told my parents, they never believed me, especially my mother. She kept arguing with my dad to send me to an asylum. Sometimes she would lock me in the closet so I wouldn't bother her. The closet was dark and small. Ghosts would surround me and...it was traumatizing. That's why I don't wanna be reminded of my ability."

I put a hand on his shoulder.

"I'm sorry your mom treated you like that."

"It's fine. I'm not living with her anymore and my dad is with his new family."

I was going to say something but I decided against it. We crossed the street when I tripped over my shoelace and caught myself by putting my hands on Michael's back.

"Hold on, I gotta tie my shoes."

He rolled his eyes and walked on. I knelt down and started tying my shoelace.

"PARIS WATCH OUT!"

I looked up and Michael tackled me into the sidewalk as a car sped by.

"What the HELL are you doing?!"

"Saving your life!"

"I'm dead, there's no life to save!"

"Oh right."

I rolled my eyes and stood up. I brushed myself off as he stood up.

"Great, now I'm dirty and my shoelaces are still untied!"

"Well sorry for forgetting!"

I sighed and was about to continue walking when I noticed the cafe.

"What?"

"The security camera."

"What?"

"There's a security camera in front of the cafe."

"Oh my God," Michael said, realizing what I was saying.

We looked at each other smiling.

"Go check the footage."

I nodded and transported into the security room. I turned on the computer but it needed a password.

"Easy."

I put in Hyun and Jin-Ae's anniversary and the security footage turned on.

"Boom."

I rewind to the night I died and watched the footage.

*8:00pm*

*Jin-Ae went outside and locked up. A person dressed in all black stepped up to her with a metal bat with their hood up. She nodded and got into her car. The person backed away. All of a sudden, he ran towards the camera, jumped, and hit it with the bat breaking it.*

The screen went black. I ran to the front of the cafe and looked up at the security camera.

"Michael, I need you. Your height is finally coming in handy."

Michael rolled his eyes and knelt down while I got on his shoulders. He stood up and I inspected the security camera. I silently cursed.

"What?"

"They destroyed it."

The person in that video planned to murder Mi-Cha and Jin-Ae was in on it.

# Chapter Fourteen

I transported us back to where Mi-Cha and Bong were waiting.

"Where were you? You've been gone for two hours."

"Remember how you said that Sung-Ho is the killer," I asked Bong.

"Yeah."

"He's the killer."

"Sung-Ho is? No, he would never do that."

"It's always the nice ones. We need to go to his house and search."

"We'll meet you there," Bong said.

"But we can just-."

"Bong is right, we'll meet you there," Michael said.

Mi-Cha and I rolled our eyes and transported to Sung-Ho's house.

"He's usually at work around this time so we don't have to worry about him."

"Do you think he did it?"

"Of course not."

"What was he like?"

"He was one of the sweetest guys I knew. He didn't use me for my fame like everyone else did but..."

"But what?"

"It somehow still got in the way. Since I'm a model, I was traveling across the world and even when I was home I always had work to do. We always argued about that and I told him we needed a break..."

She stopped talking when she realized I stopped and was staring at the car in the driveway.

*I brought out my camera and smiled.*

*"Last day in Korea."*

*I took the picture but all of a sudden I heard a scream and a loud thud. I turned around and saw a girl on the ground bleeding out and a black car driving away.*

"You were hit by a car. A black car."

Mi-Cha's eyes widened.

"Mi-Cha-."

"No, Sung-Ho wouldn't do that to me."

She ran inside the house. I sighed and followed her. I looked around the place. Damn, Koreans are rich. Was that racist? I shook my head and followed Mi-Cha into a bedroom, most likely Sung-Ho's.

"Man, I wish my bedroom looked like this. The only interesting things in my room are a Rubix cube I never solved and a poster of Ariana Grande."

"You seriously have an unhealthy obsession with her."

"Hey! I also like Zendaya and Shawn Mendes, I am open to all things."

"Trust me we know. Here's his work schedule. On the night we died-."

"He was working all night, but Bong said he wanted to meet you..."

We looked at each other.

"Aw shit," we said in unison.

My eyes widened.

"Michael!"

# Chapter Fifteen

"So how far is Jung's house?"

"Sung-Ho and not far."

"You said that ten minutes ago."

Suddenly, Mi-Cha appeared and slapped Bong.

"Woah!"

Paris appeared next to me and started looking me over.

"Are you okay?"

"I'm fine, I feel like I'm being arrested."

"That witch didn't touch you did she?"

"Who?"

"Bing Bong."

"First of all, don't ever call me Bing Bong again, second of all, what the hell did I do?"

"You murdered us."

"What?! No, I didn't!"

"Then why did you say that Sung-Ho was meeting her when he was actually at work all night?"

"Yeah! Even though I have no idea what's going on," I exclaimed.

"Because he was meeting her there, he even texted."

"Liar," Mi-Cha said.

"Okay everyone calm down, the only way to find out if she's lying is to look at Sung-Ho's texts," I said.

"Where does he work?"

"At the convenience store."

"Okay let's go then."

We started walking when my phone rang. I checked to see who it was.

"It's Chloe, I gotta take this."

"Sure go ahead and take it while we have a lead on our murder case," Paris said, annoyed.

I gave him a confused look and answered.

"Hey, babe."

"Hey, where are you?"

"I told you I'm going to be in Korea for a week."

"Oh really? Then why did Sydney call me to thank you for the letter from Paris."

Damnit, wasn't one thank you enough lady?

"Chloe-."

"Where are you and why do you even have a letter from Paris?"

"It's hard to explain."

"Try me."

"Um, well you see..."

I'm such a bad liar. I'm going to have to tell her the truth sometime. I looked at Paris and he was staring at me with hopeful eyes.

"Paris was murdered."

"Idiot," Paris said.

"What do you mean Paris was murdered?"

"Someone drowned him in his tub."

"That's impossible, the police said he overdosed. He only knew his boss there. He was alone that night, how could he be murdered?"

"I know it sounds crazy but..."

I stopped talking and my heart dropped when I realized what she just said.

"Michael?"

"How did you know he was alone that night?"

She was silent for a few moments.

"T-The police said so."

"That's not what you said Chloe," I said in a dark voice.

"Michael he was just some fucking addict that had too many, he killed himself not anyone else," she snapped.

Before I could say anything else, she hung up. I put my phone down and looked at Paris.

"Michael-."

"Like you guys said, anyone can be a suspect, even her."

I WATCHED MICHAEL WALK over to the girls. I looked down.

*"What the hell are you doing here? I told you we were done."*

*"I don't wanna be done, Paris."*

*"I'm sorry, Chlo. I just don't have feelings for you anymore. Now go home."*

*"Why?"*

*"You have a boyfriend."*

*"I don't care about him, I care about you! I love you, Paris!"*

*"No, you don't. You just find me easy to manipulate."*

*"Fuck you!"*

*"You're a psycho bitch!"*

*She slapped me. I felt my lip and it was bleeding. I glared at her.*

*"Don't talk to me or my family. Or you'll regret it."*

It's best if he doesn't know about that argument.

# Chapter Sixteen

"Baby don't worry, you are my only, you won't be lonely, even if the sky is falling down," Paris sang.

We decided to split up. Mi-Cha and Bong investigate Sung-Ho while Paris and I investigate Dong-Hyun who works in the worst place possible. A karaoke bar.

"Thank you, thank you," Paris said bowing.

Barely anyone clapped. Mostly because the guy Paris possessed couldn't sing.

"I'll have you know, that song was a hit eleven years ago."

Paris got out of the guy and sat next to me.

"When is Dong's shift supposed to start?"

"Should be any minute now."

I took a sip out of my lemonade as the next act came on. Paris slapped my back making me cough.

"There he is."

I looked over and saw a guy my height walk in.

"I see him."

"Isn't he hot?"

"I don't know how to answer that."

"Come on."

We stood up and went over to him.

"Hey, are you Dong-Hyun?"

"Yeah, who are you?"

"I'm Michael, I'm here to talk about Paris."

"What about him?"

"I just have a few questions."

Dong went over to the bar and started making drinks.

"Ask away, I'm here all night."

He seems relaxed and unstressed. Even though Paris just died four days ago.

"Paris told me you guys had a thing together."

He looked at me with wide eyes as the people at the bar started glaring at us. Right, this is Korea, not America. Even though there are still homophobic people in America, they despise it in Korea.

"Like hanging out with two girls like a double date," I said quickly.

They went back to their drinks and Dong relaxed.

"Let's talk somewhere else."

"Agreed."

We went into the bathroom and checked to see if anyone was around.

"What about me and Paris?"

"Paris told me that you were mad at him about Chloe."

"I wasn't mad."

"Liar," Paris yelled.

"I got this."

He gave me a confused look.

"Yes we got into arguments about her but that's only because he said he wanted to be with me but was still seeing her."

"How do you know?"

"I saw them talking, one day before he died."

"She was here? In Korea?"

"Yeah. After that, I broke things off with him."

"Why weren't you at his funeral then?"

"...who are you to Paris?"

"Uh well, I'm his...childhood friend."

"He's never mentioned you before."

"You said you weren't mad at him but you broke things off with him and weren't at his funeral."

"Why are you in our business?"

"Where were you that night?"

"Why do you care?"

"Why are you avoiding my questions?"

"Why are you avoiding mine? I don't even know you. For all I know you could be some creep that was all over Paris!"

"Or maybe you're a murderer!"

"Michael," Paris said.

"What's that supposed to mean? Paris overdosed."

"Unless that's what you **want** people to think. The only other people who knew about his addiction were Chloe and you, so wouldn't it be a coincidence that you broke up the night before he died?"

"Screw you."

Before I could say anything, Paris grabbed my wrist.

"Let's go."

I glared at him as Paris dragged me out.

"Why'd you drag me away? He obviously had something to do with your murder."

"We don't know that."

"He has a motive, knows where you live, and knows you had a drug problem."

"It could still be Sung-Ho, you know, the other potential murderer! He didn't even know Mi-Cha so why would he kill her? And aren't you forgetting Chloe?"

"It can't be her."

"Her motive is the same as Dong's but no it can't be her because you're in love with her!"

"Chloe isn't that type of person!"

"Oh but Dong is? You're such a hypocrite!"

"I'm a hypocrite? You knew Chloe was here and didn't tell me."

"I didn't wanna upset you."

"Well too late for that huh?"

"You just don't want it to be Chloe because then you'll have no one to fuck!"

"And maybe you don't want it to be Dong because he's the only person that doesn't wanna tear his head off around you. Oh wait, he isn't."

He glared at me with tears in his eyes. Shit, I went too far.

"Paris, I'm so-."

He started walking away.

"Where are you going?"

He ignored me and stuck his middle finger up as he walked away. I sighed. I'm such an idiot. I turned around and there was a crowd staring at me. Probably because it looked like I was arguing with myself. I awkwardly smiled at them and walked the opposite way from Paris. I didn't realize where I was going when I felt someone tug on my sleeve. I turned around and saw Bong and Mi-Cha.

"Girls, I really want to be alo-."

"Dude, shut up for two seconds," Bong exclaimed.

"Sung-Ho isn't the murderer!"

# Chapter Seventeen

"Wait, how do you know?"

Bong and Mi-Cha went into the store and saw Sung-Ho at the cash register. They went over to him.

"Hey, Sung-Ho."

"Hey Bong. I thought you wouldn't wanna see me after Mi-Cha died."

"Why wouldn't I?"

"Well, you hate me."

"I don't hate you."

"When you first met me you went ew."

"Okay, I hated you. But that's because I was overprotective of Mi-Cha."

"Why did you ignore me at her funeral then?"

"Because you were the last person she was with."

"Well, that's impossible. The last time I saw her was on our date at the cafe that morning but she had to go to work and that was the last time I saw her and my phone."

"Wait, what do you mean?"

"I went to the bathroom after she left and when I came back, my phone was gone. I told the manager and she said that she didn't see anything."

Bong and Mi-Cha looked at each other with wide eyes.

"Shit," they said in unison.

"Thanks, Sung."

"Wait, did Mi-Cha ever say anything about breaking up with me?"

"No, she was in love with you dude."

"Cool, I loved her too," he said sadly.

Bong sadly smiled at him and hugged him. He hugged back.

*"You're a good guy, Sung."*

*"Thanks, Bong. Mi-Cha looked up to you."*

*"Sung, shut up," Mi-Cha said but he couldn't hear her.*

*"What do you mean?"*

*"She hated being a model and wanted to be an artist like you. She never stopped talking about you."*

*"But I thought-."*

*"She wasn't angry at you. She was angry at your parents for always putting you down and always comparing you to her."*

*Bong looked at Mi-Cha and she was looking everywhere else instead of Bong. Bong smiled.*

*"Thanks for telling me, Sung," she said, not taking her eyes off of Mi-Cha.*

*Sung-Ho looked at what she was looking at and saw nothing. He looked back at her and nodded.*

*"No problem."*

"So, Jin-Ae stole Sung's phone and pretended to be him, asking Mi-Cha to meet him at the cafe. Jin-Ae's the murderer!"

"But why would she kill me? We don't even know each other."

"I don't know but it looks like we're gonna have to find out. But first, I need a place to sleep because it's almost midnight and I've been lugging my bookbag all day."

"Our parents are on a business trip so you can stay with me."

"Wait, where's Paris?"

"We argued and he walked away somewhere."

"I'll find him," Mi-Cha said, disappearing.

# Chapter Eighteen

After taking a breather so I wouldn't make Michael a ghost also, I went back to the karaoke bar and sat on one of the stools. I saw a drink by itself and went to drink it but then I remembered that I can't eat and drink anymore. I groaned. I miss being drunk. I felt someone sit next to me. I looked over and saw Dong.

"Well isn't this deja vu? This is how we met."

*I walked in with my bags and went straight to the bar.*

*"Um, something Korean," I said, confused.*

*"I can speak English foreigner," the bartender said.*

*"Sorry, I just got here and I'm meeting my new boss in an hour."*

*"So you have a job here in Korea and have no idea how to speak Korean?"*

*"Which is why I'm at a bar."*

*He chuckled, making me chuckle.*

*"What's your name, foreigner?'*

*"Paris."*

*He gave me a weird look.*

*"My mom wanted a girl and loves Paris."*

*"Ah. I'm Dong. What kind of drink?"*

*"Doesn't matter."*

*He smiled and started making a random drink.*

*"So, what do you do?"*

*"I'm a photographer."*

*"So if I said, "Take a picture, it'll last longer."*

*"I would flip you off."*

He softly laughed. I was about to say something else when I was cut off by someone singing horribly.

"Is a cat dying?!"

"It's a karaoke bar, there's going to be either someone who sings beautifully like Jungkook or someone who..."

"Sounds like a cat being strangled?"

"Exactly."

"So I take it you love working here," I asked sarcastically.

"Funny."

We fell into a comfortable silence.

"So, are you single?"

"Definitely."

Almost an hour later we were making out in the bathroom. My phone dinged and I checked it. It was a text from Chloe. I rolled my eyes and pulled away.

"I gotta go, can't be late on the first day."

"Wait, can I get your number?"

"Don't worry, I'll be back," I said, winking.

And I did come back. The next day, Dong showed me around Korea and taught me some Korean. As we spent more time together, we got closer. We went back to his apartment and...well, you know.

"So are you seeing someone," he asked after we finished.

"You decide to ask that after we finish," I asked out of breath.

"I'm curious."

"Nope, nobody."

"Do you want to?"

I scrunch my eyebrows together and sat up to look at him.

"Isn't same-sex relationships illegal here?"

He chucked and sat up to look at me clearly.

"No, they're not. People here...it's complicated. Some won't care but mostly everyone in Korea is homophobic."

"So, those Korean BLs?"

*He laughed.*

*"Of course, you would bring those up."*

*"What? I also watch Thai BLs."*

*We both laughed. Things were good, for a while. But, like everything in my life, it didn't last long. One day, we were walking down the street holding hands. We got looks but we didn't care. I was laughing at something Dong said but stopped when I saw her. Chloe. Dong looked worried when I stopped in my tracks and my face went pale.*

*"I'll be right back," I said angrily.*

*I went over to Chloe.*

*"What the hell are you doing here?!"*

*And we all know how that argument ended. I went back over to Dong wiping the blood off my lip.*

*"Who was she?"*

*"My crazy ex-girlfriend."*

*"I thought you said you didn't have anyone?"*

*"We broke up last week. Can we please drop it?"*

*He wanted to ask more questions but decided to drop it. But Chloe wouldn't let things go. Dong and I were on a date when I cursed silently.*

*"Great, now she's stalking me."*

*Dong turned around and saw her.*

*"Shouldn't you talk to her?"*

*"I did, you saw how that ended."*

*"Well, I'm right here if she tries something."*

*I was about to say something when Chloe sat next to me.*

*"Why," I asked annoyed.*

*"I wanna get back together."*

*"Where does your little boyfriend...Mikey think you are?"*

*"A business trip."*

*"Wow, what a coincidence, that's the same excuse you used on me when you went to sleep with him."*

*"You're drunk."*

*"Yeah, sure I am. Let's go, Dong."*

*I stood up and stumbled. I looked back at her and she was smirking.*

*"I tripped over the carpet."*

*"It's a wooden floor."*

*"Dong, let's go."*

*"Dong, did Paris tell you about his "little" problem?"*

*He looked at me confused and I grabbed his hand.*

*"He's a recovering drug addict and alcoholic. Apparently, he's been sober for thirty days, well, now back to zero days."*

*"Chloe shut up."*

*"Looks like he'll just overdose just like his good-for-nothing father."*

*I clenched my fists in anger. I grabbed my drink and threw it in her face.*

*"You fucking bitch," I yelled as Dong held me back.*

*"Hey, let's just go," he said softly.*

*I let him lead me out of there.*

*"What the hell did I see in her? And how dare she bring up my father like that?! I shouldn't have ever told her that."*

*I stopped walking when I noticed Dong wasn't beside me anymore. I turned around and saw he had stopped.*

*"What's wrong?"*

*"Nothing."*

*I gave him a confused look and we went back to my apartment. When we entered, he was still silent.*

*"Dong."*

*"When you first came to Korea, you went straight to a bar, when you were sober for thirty days and you didn't tell me that you were a recovering alcoholic."*

*"But I'm not. Before I drank every day but I don't anymore. I can handle it now."*

*"Paris-."*

*"I can," I snapped.*

"*Why didn't you tell me you were a drug addict also? Is there anything else you're hiding from me?!*"

"*What's that supposed to mean?*"

"*We've been dating for a week and I feel like I barely know anything about you!*"

"*Because I'm just going to leave anyway!*"

*He had a hurt look on his face.*

"*So what? I'm just your little fling?*"

"*That's not what I meant.*"

"*But that's what you said.*"

"*Dong-.*"

"*Let's just end this now huh?*"

*He headed towards the door and I started panicking.*

"*Dong, don't leave!*"

*He opened the door while ignoring me.*

"*I love you!*"

*He stopped.*

"*I love you. You're the only person that listened to me. Yes, I was planning on going back to my old habits when I got here but you changed me. I-I'll tell you everything okay? How my mom favors my sister over me. When I almost overdosed causing me to go to rehab. Even my dad's death just, please don't leave. You're all I have left,*" *I said sobbing.*

*He didn't say anything. The only thing you could hear was my sniffles. He turned around to look at me. I looked at him with hopeful eyes. He looked down with tears in his eyes and sighed. He looked back up with tears streaming down his face.*

"*Have a safe trip back, Paris.*"

*He closed the door, leaving me alone. I was silent for a few moments. I grew angrier as the seconds passed by. I poured my heart out to him and that's all he has to say. I dug my fingernails into my palms and screamed in anger at the door. I screamed until my lungs gave out. I fell to my knees and laid on my back, sobbing. I curled up into a ball and stayed there the whole night sobbing.*

"I'm sorry, things didn't work out. If it makes you feel better, you're very good at, well, you know," I said winking.

I stood up and went in front of him.

"You're a good guy, Dong. Whoever your soulmate is, they're very lucky."

I put my hand on his cheek but it went through him. I sighed and left. I walked down the sidewalk and kicked pebbles. It was midnight so there wasn't anyone on the street. Then, I heard footsteps behind me. I would've ignored them since they can't even see me but something didn't feel right. I stopped in my tracks and so did the footsteps. I turned around and saw a man staring at me.

"Well, hello Paris Walker,"

I was confused about how he could see me until I realized what he was.

"Exorcist," I whispered.

# Chapter Nineteen

I ran for my ghost life with the exorcist chasing me.

"Now I know how the ghosts in Ghostbusters felt!"

Mi-Cha appeared in front of me.

"There you are."

I lifted her and ran around the corner. I ran inside a building and put her down. I quickly pulled her down to the ground.

"Wha-?"

I shushed her as I heard the exorcist outside. I thought he was about to walk past but he went towards the door instead. Mi-Cha quickly transported us out in front of a house.

"Who was that?"

"An exorcist."

"What?!"

"He knew my name too. Like he was looking for me."

"Well let's get inside."

"Way ahead of you."

We walked in and saw Bong and Michael.

"Found Paris with an exorcist."

"You mean like a ghostbuster?"

Mi-Cha and I glared at him.

"Yes, Michael. Like a ghostbuster."

"We'll talk about this in the morning, Mi-Cha and I will sleep in my room while you two sleep in our parent's room."

We awkwardly looked at each other.

"Can't one of us sleep in Mi-Cha's room?"

"They turned it into a storage room."

We both sighed. After Michael got situated, he laid down next to me and turned the light off.

"Paris, I'm sorry for earlier."

"It's fine."

"No, it's not, I shouldn't have said that."

"You were right though. I make everyone I know want to tear their heads off. That's why I'm always alone."

He turned towards me.

"Paris, a lot of people care about you. Your mom, your sister, Dong, Bong, and Mi-Cha. I hate to admit this but I also care about you. Sure you can be annoying and can be sarcastic at times but that's what makes you different."

I smiled.

"Not like an "I'm not like other girls" type of way right?"

We both laughed.

"Obviously not. I know I have never said this since we met but, I'm glad you sat next to me that day."

"Me too."

We smiled at each other.

"Good night," he said, turning back around.

"Good night," I said softly.

I bit my lip as I looked down at him. I hesitantly put my hand on his shoulder making him turn around.

"What's wrong?"

I didn't answer him. I put my hands on his cheeks and kissed him.

# Chapter Twenty

Paris is kissing me. Paris. Is. Kissing. Me. I gently pushed him off.

"Paris-."

"I know, I don't know why I did that."

"I'm flattered but-."

"You're straight and dating Chloe. I know, I'm sorry. Can we just forget this happened," he asked, lying down facing away from me.

I bit my lip.

"Yeah, good night."

He stayed silent. I mentally sighed and laid down. What just happened? After a while, I fell asleep.

*I opened my eyes and I was in the back of the car with my Dad driving and Mom in the passenger seat.*

*"Dad? Mom? Where are we?"*

*They didn't answer. I looked out the window and my eyes widened when I saw we were heading to Nevada.*

*"We have to turn around!"*

*"Why, Mikey?"*

*I looked to my right and saw Paris.*

*"Is there something you're not telling us?"*

*Dad turned the radio up and my breathing picked up.*

*"Is there something you're not telling me," he asked glaring at me.*

*I heard a loud honk and I looked out my window to see a car about to barrel into us.*

*"DA-!"*

I woke up with a jolt and out of breath. I looked around and took in my surroundings. I let out a shaky breath and put my face in my hands. You're okay. You're okay. I sighed and looked up. I screeched when I saw Paris right in front of me.

"Are you okay?"

"Yeah I'm fine, why do you ask?"

"Because you're sweating and out of breath. Either you had a nightmare or you were jacking off."

"No, I would never...Yes, I had a nightmare but don't worry it was nothing."

"Are you sure?"

"Yeah. I'm sure."

"Well, Mi-Cha and Bong want to talk about our suspect list. But please shower first," he said leaving.

After he left, I sniffed myself. I do kinda smell bad. I went into the bathroom and took my clothes off. I turned on the shower and got in. Things between me and Paris are awkward now since he kissed me last night. It didn't seem like he liked me. He always seems like he's always annoyed by me. My dad told me that if someone is mean to you it means they like you. I always thought that was just a toxic thing. Like if you like someone why be mean to them? But the weirdest thing about it is that I kinda liked the kiss. But I'm straight, why would I like it? I care about Paris but I never thought about it romantically until last night. So what does that mean?

Suddenly, someone pulled the shower curtains back making me scream and cover myself.

"Stop screaming, it's just me, how long are you planning to spend in here," Bong asked, annoyed.

"I've only been in here for five minutes."

"No, you've been in here for almost an hour."

"Oh, no wonder the water's cold."

"If you don't have clothes of your own, you can borrow my dad's."

"I have clothes, please leave."

"Okay okay."

She looked down and I snapped, making her look back up.

"Hey, just because I'm a man doesn't mean you get to look down there without my permission."

"Okay geez," she said leaving.

"Yeah educate yourself."

I got out and got two towels. I wrapped a towel around my waist and went into the bedroom, drying my hair. I sat on the bed and checked my phone. I had a missed call from Chloe and my mom. I sighed and called her back. It rang a few times before she picked it up.

"Michael?"

"Yeah mom, it's me."

"Honey where have you been, I've been so worried."

Yeah, sure you were.

"How'd you get this number?"

"Chloe gave it to me. She said you were in South Korea, why would you be there?"

"I'm just...doing something."

There was a pause on the other line.

"Mom?"

"This doesn't have anything to do with your ghost stories does it?"

"Mom," I said annoyed.

"I thought you finally grew out of that but you're still a psychopath."

"I'm not crazy."

"You're having a psychotic break, do you need to-?"

"I'm not going back to that hospital mom! I'm twenty-two years old, you can't tell me what to do anymore!"

"That's no way to speak to your mother."

"No you're not, you've never been my mother. You've always treated me like a burden since I was five! Do you know what that does to a kid? It traumatizes them and you didn't fucking care! You only put me in a mental hospital when you need to be in one."

"I was only trying to help you."

"What I needed was you to support me! Why couldn't you do that? Why couldn't you just be my mother?!"

"I don't know what you want from me."

"For you to love me," I said as a tear came down my face.

"Honey I do love you."

*"I hate you so much, I wish you weren't my son."*

"...No. No, you don't. Don't call me again."

I hung up and let out a shaky breath. I called Chloe and she answered immediately.

"Hey, Chlo."

"Hey."

"Why'd you give my mom this number?"

"Why did you accuse me of murder?"

We fell into an awkward silence.

"Chlo-."

"Why are you so wrapped up in someone you don't even know?"

"It's complicated."

"Try me."

What am I supposed to tell her? 'Hey, Chloe, so Paris came back as a ghost and told me he was murdered and now I'm trying to see who killed him, oh by the way I can see ghosts.' Yeah because that **totally** doesn't sound like I need to be put in an asylum.

"It just is, I know that isn't fair to hear but I just can't explain it. Why are you trying so hard to get me off this? I thought out of all people besides Sydney you would want to find out-."

"Are you cheating on me?"

"What," I asked, completely thrown off.

"Do you have someone there in Korea and are just using Paris's death as an excuse?"

I scoffed.

"Isn't that ironic? That you did that to me?"

"N-No I didn't."

"Chloe I know you were here trying to get back together with Paris."

"That's not-."

"Chloe, for once tell me the truth!"

"Fine, I was there! Are you happy now?"

"Obviously not."

"Michael, I'm sorry."

I bit my lip as I started tearing up.

"Chloe, when I get back, we're done."

"You're dumping me? I didn't do anything!"

"Goodbye, Chloe."

I hung up before she could say anything. I groaned and ran my fingers through my still wet hair. I don't want to believe that she killed Paris but all the evidence points to her. Except for the car...The car.

*The front bumper was about to come off.*

*"What happened to his car?"*

*"I don't know."*

The car part at Paris's apartment building.

*I looked around and saw a car part on the ground.*

He was on a date with Jin-Ae that night.

*"Do you think your boss could've done it?"*

*"No, he treated me like a son. Besides, he had a date with Jin-Ae that day."*

I also noticed that the glass in the front was cracked. Like...

I quickly put my clothes on and went to the living room.

"It took you long enough-."

"Mi-Cha what was the color of the car that hit you?"

"Paris said it was black."

"Why Michael?"

"The person who killed you guys is Hyun."

# Chapter Twenty-One

***One week earlier***

Mi-Cha entered the cafe and immediately smiled when she saw Sung-Ho. She went up behind him and covered his eyes.

"Guess who?"

"Is it Bong," Sung-Ho guessed jokingly.

Mi-Cha lightly punched his arm and sat across him.

"Long time no see."

"I know, my manager had me do gigs every day but I am now free."

"Good, so how was-?"

He was cut off by Mi-Cha's phone ringing. She checked it and looked at Sung-Ho biting her lip.

"It's my manager."

"I guessed that."

"I can just call her back."

"No, go ahead, I'll be here."

Mi-Cha smiled and stood up. She kissed his cheek and went outside while answering the phone. Sung-Ho took a sip from his coffee while tapping his fingers on the table. He sighed and went to the bathroom leaving his phone on the table. Jin-Ae watched him close the door and quickly went to their table. She got it out of his bag and went back to her office. After a while, Sung-Ho returned to the table as Mi-Cha came back inside.

"I'm-."

"I'm sorry but I have to leave, is that what you're about to say," Sung-Ho asked sarcastically.

"Sung-Ho, you know how important my job is to me."

*"I know but what about me? Am I not important to you?"*

*"Babe of course you're important to me."*

*"Really? Because I always feel like your job always comes before me."*

*"Sung-Ho-."*

*"No, I'm done, Mi-Cha."*

*He grabbed his bag and left, leaving Mi-Cha alone.*

**8:10pm**

*Mi-Cha was watching a movie with Bong when her phone went off. She checked the message and it was from Sung-Ho.*

<u>*I'm sorry for earlier, can you meet me at the cafe?*</u>

*She smiled and went to put on her shoes.*

*"Where are you going?"*

*"Sung-Ho wants to meet me, bye."*

*"Wait, it's late, I'll drive you."*

*"I'll be fine, it's only to the cafe."*

*"Yeah but..."*

*"But what?"*

*"Look, I didn't wanna tell you this but I don't trust Sung-Ho."*

*"Why not?"*

*"Well you guys got together after you got famous isn't that kinda suspicious?"*

*"He's not using me, Bong. Unlike you and mom and dad."*

*"You think I'm using you? I barely give a shit about your career!"*

*"Then just stay out of my life and stop being jealous!"*

*"Oh trust me, I have nothing to be jealous of!"*

*"Good," Mi-Cha said, going to the door.*

*"And don't worry. I won't look at you. I won't speak to you. I'll stay completely out of your life. Like I always wanted."*

*Mi-Cha started tearing up and clenched her fists. She grabbed her jacket and left slamming the door.*

**Meanwhile at the airport**

Paris was playing games on his phone when the airport's intercom came on. He didn't understand Korean so he waited for them to say the announcement in English.

"All flights are canceled due to bad weather. Please come back tomorrow."

He groaned and texted Phoenix. He grabbed his bag and left. He walked to the cafe and was confused when he saw it closed. He shrugged and turned around. He pulled out his camera but Mi-Cha accidentally bumped into him.

"Sorry," she said in English.

He gave her a smile and a nod. She started crossing the street not noticing the black car speeding towards her. Paris took the picture as the car hit Mi-Cha. Paris heard her scream and then a thud. He turned around and saw the car speed off and Mi-Cha on the ground. He quickly ran to her.

"Hey, are you okay? That was a stupid question."

Paris picked her up bridal style and carried her to the sidewalk. He set her down and pulled out his phone to call 911 not noticing the black car returning. He heard a car door slam and turned around to see Hyun step out of the car.

"Hyun?"

"Step away from her Paris."

"W-Why? Why did you-?"

He pulled out a knife.

"I'm warning you, Paris."

Paris slowly stood up.

"I'll make it quick," Hyun said charging toward him.

Paris threw his camera at him hitting him in the face.

"I'm sorry," he said quickly to Mi-Cha.

He ran down the alleyway accidentally dropping his phone. Hyun was about to go after him, holding his eye when Mi-Cha grabbed his ankle.

"H-h-Hyun," Mi-Cha choked out.

*He chuckled and knelt down next to her.*

*"Oh Mi-Cha, the fame got too much for you, you just had to kill yourself," he said smiling.*

*"P-p-please-."*

*Hyun grabbed her by her hair and slit her throat, instantly killing her. He carried her and put her in the back seat and got in the car.*

*Paris ran to his apartment. He stopped to catch his breath while looking behind him. Hyun was nowhere to be seen. He quickly started feeling for his phone and cursed under his breath when it wasn't on him. He looked up when he saw headlights. He jumped out of the way and onto the ground as Hyun's car smashed into the side of the building. Paris quickly got up as Hyun stumbled out. Paris ran inside and knocked over tables as he ran upstairs.*

*He banged on the doors as he ran to his room.*

*"SOMEONE HELP ME! PLEASE!"*

*No one was coming out and he could hear Hyun coming up the stairs. He went to his door and tried to open it but it was locked. He kicked open the door and ran inside. He was about to close it but Hyun forced his way inside, knocking Paris to the floor. Paris held his hand up making Hyun stab through it causing Paris to scream out in agony. With his other hand, he grabbed a vase and smashed it against Hyun. He ran to his room and locked the door. He looked around for anything that could be used as a weapon. He found nothing as Hyun kicked the door open. He hit Paris against the head with a gun knocking him to the floor. He did this three more times and stopped. He went into the bathroom and turned on the water to clean up the blood. He went back to Paris and stopped when he heard a voice outside.*

*"Paris!"*

*Outside, Chloe was looking at Paris's window. Paris weakly opened his eyes.*

*"Chloe," he said under his breath.*

*"I'm sorry for earlier! Can we talk?"*

*Hyun cursed and went to the door.*

*"Don't."*

*Hyun stopped in his tracks.*

*"Please," he said weakly.*

*Hyun went to him.*

*"Not dead yet?"*

*Hyun turned off the lights and grabbed Paris by his hair. He dragged him to the now full tub and held his head under the water until he went completely still. He brought him back up and let go causing Paris's lifeless body to fall to the floor.*

*"This is what happens when you try to play hero."*

# Chapter Twenty-Two

"So, Hyun murdered us," I asked.

"Yeah."

"He's the murderer?"

"Seems like it."

I ran a hand through my hair and stood up.

"I'm gonna get some air."

"There's air in here."

"I obviously said that so I can be alone," I snapped at her.

I left slamming the door. I started pacing and biting my nails. I heard the door open and looked up to see Michael.

"You wanna go for a walk?"

I nodded and we started walking down the street not speaking.

"We need proof," I said, breaking the silence.

Michael pulled out his phone and put it up to his ear to make it look like he was talking to someone.

"What were you thinking?"

"We could go to Hyun or Jin-Ae's place but he only used a knife and gun and he most likely threw those away. They're going to get away with it."

"Paris, we're going to catch those bastards, they're not going to get away with this."

"Why don't you hate me?"

"Am I supposed to hate you?"

"I kissed you last night, you should hate me."

"Paris I would never hate you for that."

I opened my mouth to say something but stopped when I made eye contact with the exorcist from last night.

"Shit," I yelled.

I grabbed Michael's hand and started running with him right behind us.

"Why are we running?!"

I didn't answer him as we ran into a mall. I pulled him into a large crowd.

"We need to split up."

"What's going on?"

"The exorcist from last night is here, he's after me so you need to act normal and get away from me."

"But-."

"If he sees you with me then he'll know that you can see me, now go!"

HE DISAPPEARED AND I pushed my way out of the crowd bumping into someone.

"Sorry!"

"Move!"

The guy pushed me out of the way and looked around like he was looking for someone. The Exorcist. It's okay because Paris probably went back to the house.

"?? ???."

I looked where he was looking and he was looking straight at Paris. Great. He started going to him but I tripped him, making him fall. He looked straight at me and glared at me.

"? ?? ??," he sneered.

I don't know what he said but I probably should run. I ran up the escalator as he chased me. As long as he doesn't know I'm not a ghost, it should be fine. But of course, I just had to bump into someone and fall.

"? ???, ????!"

"I'm okay really," I said as more people started staring.

Someone helped me up.

"Oh thank you."

I screeched when I saw it was the exorcist. He dragged me away from the crowd and to a small excluded area.

"??? ??? ? ? ????, ??? ? ? ?????"

"Sorry no Espanol," I said nervously.

"You can see them," he said in English.

"Okay, that I can understand."

"Answer me!"

"I don't know what you're talking about psycho!"

"I saw you talking to that ghost, I saw you look at him, that's why you tripped me."

"I tripped you by accident."

"Then why'd you run?"

"Your face is so ugly it scared me so I ran."

He scoffed.

"You really think I'm dumb don't you?"

"Who even are you?"

"I'm Byung-Woo and I'm going to make sure your little ghost friends disappear for good."

"Good luck with that," I said sarcastically.

All of a sudden, he was knocked out by a baseball bat. He fell to the ground revealing Paris behind him.

"Where'd you get the bat?"

"The sports section."

He grabbed my hand and transported us to an alley.

"I'll never get used to that. Where are we?"

"I don't know, I just transported us to a random alley."

I looked at our hands intertwined and blushed. I looked back up at Paris and he was looking around but I could only focus on him. His piercing blue eyes, his beautiful face. My heart started pounding. Why am I feeling this way?

"I think we're good," he said, turning to me.

I didn't say anything, still entranced.

"Michael?"

I snapped back into reality.

"Uh, handsome."

I mentally face palmed as he gave me a confused look.

"Nothing um, let's just-."

I accidentally bumped into someone as I was leaving the alley.

"Sorry!"

He cursed in Korean as he started picking up his papers. I started helping him but he slapped my hand away.

"You stupid foreigners, don't you know not to touch other people's stuff," he said in English.

"Sorry."

He hurried off. Paris put a hand on my shoulder and squeezed it.

"That's Hyun."

# Chapter Twenty-Three

I started going towards him when Michael stopped me.

"Don't."

"Why not?"

"He can't see you."

"Fine, you can beat him up."

"We don't have any proof. Do you know where he lives?"

I nodded and transported us there. Michael looked around shocked.

"Damn, he's rich."

"Well he was a famous photographer but his reputation got...ruined..."

We stopped in our tracks.

"By who?"

"Bong and Mi-Cha's parents."

"A motive."

'Now we just need to prove it."

"I'll get Mi-Cha and Bong."

"Wait, don't leave me at-."

HE TRANSPORTED AWAY.

"At the creepy murderer's house."

I looked back at the house. His car wasn't in the driveway so he wasn't home thank God. I went to the window since he would obviously lock his door and tried to open it. Of course, I didn't realize that the windows would be locked too. I can't just break it because then he'll know. I went around the back and saw an open window on the second floor. I climbed up the tree next to his house but I was still kinda far away.

I took a deep breath and jumped across to the window barely making it. I held onto the edge of the window for dear life as I dangled. I lifted myself and climbed into the room but fell on top of a desk right at the window causing me to fall to the ground. I groaned in pain. I stood up holding my arm. I looked around and I was in a small bedroom. This is probably Hyun's room. Well of course he lives alone. There was an awful smell in the air as my phone rang.

"Hello?"

"Hey, it's Bong. We're at the cafe."

"I thought you were coming here?"

"We are. Mi-Cha and Paris are getting the tape from last night. We also wanted to ask Jin-Ae some questions but she isn't here."

"Do you think she ran," I asked looking around the room.

"I don't know."

I looked at the ground and my heart dropped. There was a blood trail leading to the closet. I ignored Bong calling my name and made my way to the closet. I shakingly opened the door and fell to the ground, shocked and yelling. In the closet was Jin-Ae's decaying corpse.

"S-she's here."

"Jin-Ae?"

"Yeah, s-she's dead."

I didn't hear what she said next because after I said that, I heard the front door slam. Hyun's back.

# Chapter Twenty-Four

Hide. I need to hide right now. Hyun was coming up the stairs fast. The only place to hide was under the bed so I quickly crawled under and waited. I heard him open the door and come inside the room. He stopped at the closet. I forgot to close the closet. He scoffed.

"??? ??? ?? ?????"

It was quiet for a few seconds before I heard a thud and Jin-Ae's corpse fell to the ground. Her dead eyes staring right at me. I covered my mouth, gagging and tearing up as he smashed a hammer against her head repeatedly, splashing blood on my face.

"??? ????, ?? ???.??? ?? ??? ???"

What's he even saying? There was silence as I laid on the floor waiting for him to leave.

"? ??? ?? ????? ??."

My blood turned cold. I don't know what he said but the way he said it made my skin crawl. He went around the bed.

"??? ?? ??? ? ?????"

There was a moment of silence.

"?, ??? ??????."

All of a sudden, he grabbed my feet and dragged me out from under the bed.

"Found you," he said, smiling wickedly.

I looked up at him scared.

"Why are you in our business? I don't even know you."

I didn't answer. Knowing what he's done, he's so much scarier up close. He tilted his head and smirked.

"Are you scared of me?"

He knelt down to my level and chuckled. I wrapped my hand around my phone as he lifted my chin to look directly at him.

"Who are you?"

I smashed my phone against his eye making him scream in pain. He held his eye, giving me enough time to run out of the room. I ran down the stairs to the front door and tried to open it but it was locked from the outside.

"It's just you and me," I heard him yell from upstairs.

"Michael."

I turned around and saw Paris waving me over to a closet. I ran inside and he closed the door. He grabbed my hand and transported us out of there. I didn't know where we were but I couldn't breathe. Paris guided me somewhere and we sat down still holding hands.

"It's okay, I won't let him hurt you okay, I promise."

I looked into his eyes.

"I promise."

I leaned in and hugged him and he hugged back. I don't know how we're going to prove that Hyun is the murderer but right now I feel safe in Paris's arms.

# Chapter Twenty-Five

We waited for Mi-Cha and Bong to come back. Michael was still in my arms shivering. I knew I should've gone with him. After a while, he pulled away and wiped his eyes.

"I'm sorry."

"Hey, don't apologize. What happened in there?"

"I was hiding under the bed when he started smashing Jin-Ae's head multiple times and he knew I was under there. But..."

His eyes widened.

"I left my phone there."

"I'll go get it."

I was about to leave when he grabbed my arm and looked at me with pleading eyes.

"I'll be right back."

He nodded and let go. I transported to Hyun's house. I looked around for his phone and saw Jin-Ae's corpse on the ground.

"That bastard," I said angrily.

I looked around and saw his phone on the floor cracked. I picked it up and was about to transport when I noticed that it was recording. Michael must've accidentally recorded the whole...thing. Michael you genius! I transported back to Michael and immediately hugged him. He hugged back confused.

"I thought you would get tired of hugging me by now," he joked.

"You recorded him admitting it."

"I did?"

"We just have to give this to the police and everything will go back to normal!"

"Yeah, normal," he said sadly, smiling.

I wanted to ask him why he wouldn't be happy but decided not to.

WE WATCHED THEM ARREST Hyun and take him away in cuffs.

"Finally, this is over," Mi-Cha said.

Then, Hyun looked straight at me and gave me the most wicked smile that sent chills down my spine. Something doesn't feel right. Why would he be-?

"Now that that's over, we should celebrate," Paris said.

"Your ghosts, how can you celebrate," Bong asked.

Paris and Mi-Cha smirked at each other.

I knew they were thinking about karaoke.

"Walk through fire for you, just let me adore you," they sang in unison.

They had possessed the worst singers in this bar.

"Well you must be happy to return to your girlfriend," Bong said.

"She's not my girlfriend anymore. We broke up."

"Why?"

"We just...didn't work out."

"Is that the reason? Or is it because you fell in love with someone else," Bong said motioning towards Paris.

I cleared my throat.

"P-Paris? No, we're just friends."

"I never said Paris's name," she said teasingly.

"??? ? ? ? ??? ?? ??? ??," the employee said.

"?? ??," Bong yelled, raising my hand.

"What?! Bong, I can't sing!"

"Neither can they, now get up there, lover boy."

She pushed me onto the stage.

"?? ???"

"Um."

I looked at Paris.

"Beautiful...b-by Bazzi ft Camila Cabello."

He nodded and played the song. I cleared my throat.

*Hey*

*Beautiful beautiful beautiful beautiful angel*

*Love your imperfections every angle*

*Tomorrow comes and goes before you know*

*So I just had to let you know*

*The way that Gucci look on you amazing*

*But nothing can compare to when you naked*

*Now a backwood and some Henny got you faded*

*You're saying you're the one for me I need to face it*

I hope Paris understands why I chose this song. But then I noticed that he wasn't with the girls anymore. I looked down sadly.

*Tomorrow comes and goes before you know*

*So I just had to let you know*

I was about to give the microphone back when I heard singing behind me.

**Oh my God, where did the time go?**

**I wished the hours would go slow**

**How is it 6 AM?**

**Your touch is hindsight**

**Beautiful beautiful sight right now**

**Beautiful beautiful life right now**

**Got the angel saying the word right now like**

**Oh-Ah**

Paris had possessed a good singer but I saw past them and only saw Paris.

**I thank God for my lucky stars**

**Darling, don't you know what you are?**

**Yeah Michael you are**

I blushed at that and we sang the chorus in unison. We got closer as we sang and looked into each other's eyes. It was like we were the only two in the room. I never wanted this feeling to end.

"I just had to let you know," I sang.

"Swear to God you're beautiful," Paris sang, getting closer.

I started leaning in but stopped when I noticed he wasn't in the person's body anymore. I snapped back into reality when I heard everyone clapping and cheering. I looked around and saw Paris go outside. I followed him and saw him waiting for me. We didn't say anything for a while. I let out a shaky breath and went towards him. I cupped his face and kissed him. He kissed back and put his hands on my waist. We pulled away out of breath. I looked into his eyes, tearing up.

"I love you."

He pushed a strand of hair out of my face smiling.

"I love you too."

# Chapter Twenty-Six

I woke up to the whole blanket on top of me. I sat up stretching and noticed that the other side of the bed was empty and Paris wasn't in the room. My heart shattered.

"No, no, no!"

He can't be gone! I didn't get to say goodbye. I ran around the house looking for him and saw him on the couch writing something. He looked up and saw me. He immediately smiled.

"Hey, I didn't wanna wake you so-."

I cut him off by hugging him.

"What's wrong?"

"I thought you moved on."

"Sorry for scaring you, but it is weird why I'm still here."

"Where's Mi-Cha and Bong?"

"I don't know, maybe they're still asleep, it is five am."

I thought about Hyun smirking at me.

"Doesn't something feel off to you?"

"No," he said, not looking up from the paper.

"What are you doing?"

"Just writing a goodbye letter to you."

"But I'm right here."

"For you to remember me bye."

I looked down sadly. I felt him grab my hand and guide me to the couch.

"Look, I'm sorry I brought you into this."

"What do you mean?"

"I mean...I just wish we never met."

My heart shattered. He must've noticed the heartbroken look on my face.

"I didn't mean it like that."

"But you still said it," I said, ripping my hand away from his grip.

I stood up and started going to my room.

"Michael, it's going to be okay."

"How? Tell me how it's going to be okay, Paris! I'm never going to see you again after everything we've been through! How is any of this okay?!"

"...it's not."

I looked back up at him with tears streaming down my face.

"You're right. We never should've met," I said immediately regretting it.

My heart broke even more when I saw the hurt on his face when I said that. I shook my head and went to my room slamming the door. I slid down the door and heard a whoosh meaning he left. That's when I broke down. Why did I say that? I'm so stupid. I felt myself hyperventilating. I grabbed my pillow and put it on my face muffling my screams.

I SAT AT THE CAFE PLAYING with my fingers. He didn't mean it. He just needs some space. I was in the security room playing with the tapes. Some people are crazy here. I accidentally went to the tape on the night I died and groaned. I was about to stop it when I noticed something. Jin-Ae is in the car. Jin-Ae is in Hyun's car. Then, who's the woman locking...up?

I felt my stomach drop as I zoomed in.

*"Did she say who murdered her?"*

*"He was working all night. But Bong said he wanted to meet me..."*

*"Because he was meeting you there. He even texted!"*

She was confident of Sung-Ho being the murderer.
*"He knew my name. Like he was looking for me."*
*"We'll talk about this in the morning."*
She was dismissive when I told them about the exorcist and didn't say a word when we found out Hyun murdered us. Hyun didn't know I came back as a ghost, only she did. She would be innocent because she was just her sister. She knew that Hyun hated their family so he could get his revenge. So he can do all the work and she wouldn't get caught. It was her this whole time. She planned Mi-Cha's murder.

Michael. I went to transport when I felt something hit my head making everything black.

# Chapter Twenty-Seven

I woke up groaning. What the hell? I tried to stand up but I was bound to a chair which is impossible since I'm dead. I looked around and I was in a dark room and the chair was surrounded by a red circle.

"Oh shit," I mumbled to myself.

"Paris?"

I looked to my left and saw Mi-Cha in the same position.

"Mi-Cha, I don't want to scare you but I saw this happen in The Conjuring," I said nervously.

"I can't believe Bong would do this to me."

"People will do anything out of jealousy. But, this honestly doesn't seem like Bong. Then again, I've only known her for a day."

"We've been here for four days, Paris."

"Damn really?"

"That exorcist guy said that he's going to get rid of us at 3 AM."

"What time is it now?"

"I think one in the afternoon."

"Michael will piece it together by then."

"What if Bong tries to get rid of him too?"

"Then I'll break out of these ropes and kill her myself."

"And if he doesn't piece it together and leaves?"

"Then we're screwed and I will come back to life and kill him."

I ZIPPED UP MY LAST suitcase. Paris has been gone the whole morning. I overreacted and went too far. Now I might not get to say goodbye.

"Michael."

I jumped at Bong's voice. I sighed in relief.

"Bong, you scared me."

"Sorry, are you leaving for America?"

"Yeah, my flight leaves in an hour. Have you seen Paris?"

"No. I...said goodbye to Mi-Cha when she moved on."

"...fuck," I whispered tearing up.

He's gone.

"I'm sorry. I know how you felt about him."

"Thanks, Bong. I'm sorry about Mi-Cha."

"It's fine. My parents are most likely going to make me a model when they come back."

"But you're nineteen."

"It's different in Korea, you still have to listen to your parents."

"That sucks."

"Yeah, Sung-Ho even sent me this," she said, giving me a card.

It was a cheesy good luck card. I chuckled. Then, I saw the date was the day before Paris and Mi-Cha died. I looked at her confused.

"I don't get it," I said smiling slightly.

"Oh, the Korean means Good Luck."

"I know that part but he gave this the day before Mi-cha died."

"So?"

"So, how could he know you would be taking over Mi-Cha's career? I mean none of this even happened until..."

My heart dropped as she smiled at me. Oh my God. I gulped and fake chuckled.

"He probably got the date wrong. I do that a lot too," I said, giving her the card back.

"Yeah, I can tell."

"Um, how far away is the airport from here?"

"Like thirty minutes."

"I better get going then," I said, grabbing my bag.

"It was nice meeting you, Michael," she said, hugging me.

I hesitantly hugged back.

"You too."

I pulled away and gave her a small smile. I left and immediately ran to the cafe. I ran inside out of breath causing everyone to look at me. I looked around for Paris or Mi-Cha.

"Shit."

I ran out and ran to Paris's apartment.

"Paris! Mi-Cha! PARIS!"

Shit. Shit. Shit! Where are they?

"I could help you."

I turned around and saw the ghost of Jin-Ae.

"Jin-Ae?"

She nodded.

"You know where they are?"

She nodded.

"Follow me."

I followed her for about an hour until we got to an abandoned house surrounded by grass.

"Yeah this definitely doesn't look like a place where people get murdered," I said sarcastically.

She shushed me and we went around the back. She went through the door and unlocked it.

"Teamwork," I said, raising my hand for a high five.

She ignored it and went on. Ouch. We went downstairs to the basement and saw Paris and Mi-Cha tied up.

"Guys!"

"Michael, no!"

I was about to ask why when everything went black.

# Chapter Twenty-Eight

*"Michael."*

*I woke up to my mom calling me.*

*"Are we there yet?"*

*"Only a few more hours."*

*Then, why'd you wake me up?*

*"Look at the mountains."*

*I looked out the window as dad turned up the radio.*

*"Woah."*

*All of a sudden, I heard a loud honk. Before I could do anything, a large truck smashed into us knocking me out.*

My head was killing me as I felt myself being dragged. I heard Paris yelling but it was muffled as my breathing became more shallow. I closed my eyes letting darkness take over me.

*I woke up in pain.*

*"Mom? Dad?"*

*I looked around and I was still in the car but it was upside down, totaled and I was alone. It was pitch black outside and freezing.*

*"MOM?! DAD?!"*

*I started panicking. I quickly unbuckled my seatbelt and crawled to the door. I opened it and fell out. I stood up and shivered because of the cold. I started walking even though I had no idea where I was going. I decided to go back to the car but it was gone. I started crying.*

*"Mommy," I whispered.*

*Then, I saw a bright light. I started going to it when someone grabbed my arm. I turned around and it was a girl my age but she had dark circles around her eyes and was very pale.*

*"Follow me."*

*I followed her for a while. I was about to ask where we were going when I heard yelling. I looked forward and saw my parents arguing with someone with the police. I smiled.*

*"Mom! Dad!"*

*I ran towards them but the girl stopped me. She shook her head. She took me to the ambulance and I saw myself. That's impossible, I'm right here. She turned me around and made me lay on top of myself.*

*"Wake up."*

I woke up to darkness. I sat up holding my head. Where am I? I stood up and tried to make out my surroundings. I walked forward and immediately hit my head on the door. I held my forehead groaning. I felt around for the doorknob and tried to open it but it was of course locked. I sighed.

"I see you're awake," I heard a voice from the other side of the door say.

"Byung-Woo?"

"Actually it's Sung-Ho."

"Wait you're in on this too? Why?"

"Because Bong will quickly become a famous model since her famous sister died. And when Bong marries me, I can finally quit that stupid job and we'll be rich."

"...couldn't you just do that with Mi-Cha?"

"Her parents didn't want her to marry me."

"And what makes you so sure that Bong will change anything?"

"Because we're going to get married before her parents come back. We just need to get rid of you and your ghoulfriends."

"Just let us go."

He scoffed and I heard him walk away. I pounded on the door. This closet is too small. Don't go back there, Michael. You have to save Paris and Mi-Cha. I started pacing. I turned back around and stopped when I saw a girl my age but she looked familiar.

"It's you. From that day."

She nodded.

"You're not a ghost because you were little then and now you're-."

"I am a ghost, I'm just stuck here because of him."

"Byung?"

"I age and feel pain like I'm alive but no one can see me."

"That day, I died. How'd you save me?"

"I just led you back to your body. It wasn't your time. I'm sorry you can see us because of me."

"Wait so Byung and Bong, they both-?"

"No, their families have the ability and were passed on to them but they can't see me since he "exorcised" me."

"So he exorcised you, but it went wrong so you're still here...but in pain."

"It went wrong for all of us."

All of a sudden, a bunch of ghosts appeared, freaking me out.

"It's okay, they won't hurt you. We want to make a deal."

"What kind of deal?"

"We'll help you save your friends if you save us."

"How?"

"Byung wears a necklace around his neck, it has our souls in it. All you need to do is break the necklace. You need to hurry because he'll exorcise your friends in ten minutes."

"Well, how do I beat all three of them without getting my ass whooped again?"

"Leave that to us."

WE WATCHED HIM THROW holy water around while chanting something in Korean. I looked at the clock and it was five minutes to three. Michael is gonna die if we don't do something.

"Mi-Cha, use your long nails and get us out of here."

She glared at me.

"Even if we do, we can't leave because of that stupid circle."

I sighed.

"I'm sorry," Mi-Cha said.

"What do you mean?"

"If you hadn't tried to save me that night and if I hadn't been dumb enough to go-."

"Mi-Cha, I don't regret helping you. Even if I knew this would happen, I would do it again."

"?????."

"...I don't know what that means."

"It means I love you, idiot."

"Oh well, ????? to you too."

I looked over at Bong and for a split second, I saw sympathy and regret in her eyes. Then, I thought of an idea.

"Mi-Cha, talk to your sister," I whispered.

"Why? She set this whole thing up."

I looked at Sung-Ho.

"Maybe she didn't. What was the last thing she said to you that night?"

"She was trying to warn me about...Sung-Ho."

"Maybe you can convince her to help us."

"How?"

All of a sudden, we heard a crash upstairs. We were all down here and that didn't sound like Michael breaking out.

# Chapter Twenty-Nine

I heard footsteps walk past the door. One of the ghosts unlocked the door and I quietly went into the hallway. I grabbed the bat beside the door that one of the ghosts left and crept up behind Byung. I swung the bat and hit him against his head making him fall to the floor with a heavy thud. I heard footsteps coming up the stairs. I quickly ripped the necklace off of Byung and crushed it under my feet. I heard whooshing sounds and the girl smiled at me as she glowed.

"Thank you."

She knocked over one of the candles onto the carpet creating a fire.

"Get your friends and hurry."

She disappeared. I turned around and saw Sung-Ho.

BONG STARTED TO FOLLOW Sung-Ho upstairs.

"Bong, wait! I know you don't wanna do this," Mi-Cha said.

"I have no choice."

"Yes, you do."

"They were going to kill you regardless and if I tried to stop them they would've killed me too. That's why I tried to stop you that night. I was hoping that maybe we could think of something but...that's no excuse. I'm sorry, I'm such a bad sister."

"No, you're not."

"Are you sure," I asked whispering.

"Sh. Sung-Ho was right, I do look up to you. I love how you stand up to mom and dad when they try to change you. Which is why you need to stand up now and be my big sister."

Bong started pacing. Then, I started smelling smoke from upstairs. Shit.

"Come on, babe," I said.

"Don't call me that."

"Sorry."

She sighed. She looked at us biting her nails.

"Please," Mi-Cha said pleading.

After a while, Bong nodded and grabbed some water. She scrubbed away a part of the circle. She was about to untie us when we heard footsteps coming down the stairs. We looked up and saw Sung-Ho and his head was split open.

"You bitch!"

Then, Michael tackled him down the rest of the stairs.

"Bong, untie us now," I said.

SUNG-HO PUNCHED ME knocking me down and got on top of me. He put his hands around my neck and started choking me. I tried to get out of his grip but he was too strong. I started seeing spots and dug my fingers into his eyes making him scream in agony and squeeze harder. Then, he was off of me and I gasped for air. I looked up and saw Paris with the bat from upstairs. He dropped it and immediately hugged me. I hugged back tearing up. I pulled away.

"I didn't mean-."

"I know, it's okay."

We smiled and kissed. We pulled away and rested our foreheads against each other.

"Hey, I don't wanna ruin your moment but the house is still on fire," Bong said sarcastically.

"Right, I forgot about that."

We stood up as the fire started spreading down here and smoke surrounded us. Paris and Mi-Cha quickly grabbed our hands and teleported us out to the yard.

"Do you think Byung and Sung-Ho will be okay?"

Then, there was an explosion making us fall.

"Yeah, they definitely didn't make it."

Then, we heard sirens behind us.

"This happens in every horror movie. The cops take their sweet time until everyone is dead," Paris complained.

Two officers stepped out of the vehicle.

"???? ??? ?? ??? ? ??? ????? ??? ???? ???-."

"??? ???. ?? ?? ?? ??? ???.? ???? ?? ?? ????? ? ?? ?? ?? ??? ?????, ?? ??? ?? ?? ??? ?? ????? ????."

"What are they saying," Paris asked Mi-Cha.

"Bong is turning herself in," Mi-Cha said in disbelief.

"Ma'am ??? ??????"

"?."

"...??, ??? ??? ??? ?? ??????. ???? ???? ??? ?? ????? ??? ??????."

They handcuffed her and started taking her away.

"Officer, please be easy on her."

He ignored me and took her to the back of the car. Bong looked at us with tearful eyes. She smiled while crying and got in the car.

"Um...sir, do you need to be checked by the...," the other officer asked in English.

"Oh no, I'm fine."

Not really but it'll be okay.

# Chapter Thirty

"Your flight leaves at seven and my parents get home at six-thirty so be out of the house by then," Mi-Cha said handing me my ticket.

"I will. Don't worry."

She sighed and hugged me. I hugged back tightly.

"I'm gonna miss you."

"Me too."

"Please don't forget to visit Bong."

"I won't."

We separated and she went to Paris.

"I still think we're soulmates," Paris said.

"You're boyfriend's right there."

"I meant platonically dummy."

"Oh then yeah we're platonic soulmates."

They hugged and Mi-Cha started glowing. They separated as she started disappearing.

"I'll see you on the other side," she said smiling.

A few seconds later she disappeared. Paris sat on the floor and I sat next to him.

"What do you think the other side is like?"

"I don't know, I can only see ghosts."

He softly laughed and I sadly smiled while tearing up. I looked away as my tears fell.

"Hey," he said softly, turning my head towards him.

I looked into his blue eyes and they were glistening with tears.

"I'm happy that you're moving on. You deserve to be at peace but, I'm just gonna miss you."

"I know, I'm gonna miss you too. But I want you to move on, okay? I want you to live your life, get married, and have kids. Just promise me...that you won't forget me."

"I could never forget you."

He chuckled.

"Cheesy until the end huh?"

"And you're sarcastic until the end."

We softly laughed while holding hands. Then, he started glowing. We looked at each other with tears streaming down our faces.

"I love you," I said.

"I know, I love you too."

We kissed and pressed our foreheads together as he started disappearing. I cried even harder. He wiped away my tears and I looked into his bright blue eyes one last time.

"Close your eyes okay?"

I nodded and closed my eyes as he pressed a kiss on my forehead. I heard a soft "I love you" and then I felt nothing. I didn't wanna open my eyes but I had to. I opened my eyes and Paris was gone. Paris was gone from my life forever.

I sat in my seat on the plane and looked out the window as we took off. I laid my head against the window and was about to drift off to sleep when I noticed an envelope sticking out of my bag. I got it out and it was marked: *To Mikey, from yours only.*

I smiled and opened it.

*Dear Mikey,*

*I'm terrible at writing letters but I wanted to leave you something to remember me bye. I know you were annoyed by me at first and I thought you were a dick also. But as we got to know each other these past few days, I fell in love with you. I just want you to know that I'm not scared of moving on. I'm just scared of leaving you there alone. You made me feel alive again. I just wanna let you know that I love you. I really fucking love you. Maybe we'll meet each other in the next life. Goodbye Michael. Thank you for loving me. Thank you for making me feel alive again. I want you to continue living your life but promise me one thing. Please remember me.*

*Love, Paris*

Don't worry, I will. I promise.

# Epilogue

I have been able to see ghosts since I was five years old. I used to be afraid of them but then I learned that they used to be living human beings just like us who just wanna be at peace. They just wanna see their loved ones one last time and complete what they need to do so they can move on to the afterlife. Two ghosts, in particular, helped me realize that.

Mi-Cha helped me realize that you shouldn't hold grudges against people and forgive them.

Paris helped me realize to not be afraid of ghosts. He helped me realize what love really is.

I don't know what happens in the afterlife when we move on, but I hope they're at peace and maybe we'll see each other again in the next life. But for now, I will keep my promise to Paris and live my life. I'll never forget him. I promised.

## The End

# Don't miss out!

Visit the website below and you can sign up to receive emails whenever DeJane Penick publishes a new book. There's no charge and no obligation.

https://books2read.com/r/B-A-MVJR-IUIAC

**BOOKS2READ**

Connecting independent readers to independent writers.

www.ingramcontent.com/pod-product-compliance
Lightning Source LLC
Chambersburg PA
CBHW031429130726
47989CB00003B/1071